A Gothic Rendezvous

J.L. Baumann

Printed in The United States of America
Link Printing, Groveland, Florida 34736

No part of this publication may be reproduced in whole or in part, or stored in a retrieval system, or transmitted in any form or by any means, electronic, mechanical, photocopying, recording, or otherwise, without written permission from the publisher. For information regarding permission, write to Post Mortem Publications, 146 East Broad Street, Groveland, FL 34736, or E-Mail:

Contact@Postmortempublications.com

Copyright: ©Post Mortem Publications 2015
All rights reserved

ISBN 978-1-941880-38-8

~ First Edition ~

Table of Contents

Elizabeth	3
A Lighter Experience	5
Bon Voyage	7
Ex Libris	9
Embrace Your Fate	11
Ooh La La	13
The Science of Slavery	15
A Solitary Tree	17
Trick or Treat	19
Undying Love	21
Heed Indeed	23
Expose Yourself	25
Nighty Night	27
Decisions	29
Severed	31
I Ain't An Ant!	33
Passion	35
Allured	37
Just One Look	39
Souplexed	41
An Amicable Resolution	43
The Internet Cowboy	45
Malaise	47
Love's Demands	49

Elizabeth

Her hair was raven black, her skin was alabaster
But crimson is her color, you only had to ask her
A single rose she wore, assigned in contradiction
To places felt ignored, for attentive recognition

For placed within her locks, it denoted regal grace
But like the crimson fox, it was never in one place
Sewn on black silk ribbon, secure around her neck
It called to all submission, for passionate respect

The rose of red professed, surrender to the night
When laid upon her breast, of satin pearly white
I am the queen of hearts, she verily proclaimed
Submit or now depart, for to me it's all the same

But if you stay I warn you, you'll be in my domain
Where a heart of crimson roses, is never ever tame

A Lighter Experience

You heard it from the other room
It began with a pat pat pat
To the bottom of the pack
Upon the Formica kitchen table
The crinkle of the cellophane
The tearing of the paper
An overture to that familiar ching
The flint wheel lit the flame
While the inhalation sucked it in
Above the crackle of the lit tobacco
The sound of satisfaction was exhaled
And then the metal lid snapped closed

Bon Voyage

The   now
Attic
Pussycats
It has wooden a floor
This time the trunk is back
Three new stickers naturally
Black behind brass hinges
Locked up and secure
Safe from the cats
Party time!

      T   d
    a   n
  i   e
    l s

Ex Libris

Blue eyes twinkled as they opened
And saw the void
Their head was in a wicker basket
That sat upon a feathered bed

They peered about as if annoyed
And wondered why they were not dead
Is that a cactus that I see?
The head thought
Is that a flower? How could it be?
With all those thorns about?

The leafless tree that threw no shadow
Anywhere was silent
I asked it how it had got to be
It only stood there in-compliantly

A lizard here, a lizard there, a landscape
That was not so bare
That I had felt that I was all alone

There was a fly that had no wings
A rusted car that lacked the things
To make it go

There was a lover's heart which beat itself
Upon a rock with such conviction
That it never, ever, ever stopped

There was a noise throughout the air
It was hard to hear, but it was there
It was a song that had no ear to make it be
Discordantly it dared to sing for all eternity

A wafting smell had caught my eye's attention
It smelled of bread

I do not know if you have been here long
But as for me, - I arrived by chicken

Embrace Your Fate

I'm soft and I'm furry and I'm not in a hurry
The little bunny said to me
I won't even struggle when I get a snuggle
As verily soft as soft can be
But carrots beware of this ravenous hare
I'll eat you most deliciously
But as you well know, we all have to go
Really, not much differently
So whenever I lunch on carrots a bunch
I do completely reverently
See I know all along my carcass belonged
To the local glove factory

Ooh La La

There is nothing like a French girl to make a boy a man
Especially in springtime when Chauvin makes his stand
To feel the conquest of desire, within his heart he tries
To find the right selection, a fancy to his eyes

He banters all about the town to find a medal for his chest
For there is no way he wants to settle, for a second best
He wonders just exactly how much it's going to take
To sacrifice naiveté, -his dignity at stake

He chooses trepidatiously and hopes she won't discover
His undisclosed ineptitude, his weakness as a lover
With charm and femininity, with softness to the touch
Her scent has overcome him, he surrenders in the clutch

He'll never be the same again, he'll know no greater joy
For there is nothing like a French girl to make a man a boy

The Science of Slavery

I was compromised beyond my will to be
It had crept inside me, while I was asleep
Each day it took a little task away from me
My constitution ran away without a peep

At first I thought it would enhance my state
For I could go beyond my physical plane
Transform myself above my worldly fate
To leave behind my cumbersome complaints

It isn't the alcohol that I cannot resist
It isn't cigarettes or food that beckons me
It's not cocaine or crack I must insist
Insidiously, I was corrupted most acceptably

So being the jailer that has me locked inside
If I pull the plug, will only my computer die?

A Solitary Tree

I saw a barren tree, alone upon a hill
Gnarled and twisted, it before the wind
Defiantly, in solitude, it stood still
Its spirit had no power to rescind
To bargain and regain its youth
For after all, it is the simple truth

Tenaciously, it weathered wind and rain
Its youthful beauty there for all to see
Alone, she lorded over her domain
Which did not bear another single tree
For miles around, she was the only one
A barren beacon, she had now become

For fifty years she flourished in her prime
Adored by all who sought her pulchritude
They came for inspiration all the time
To write of love in terms of certitude
Her doubtless majesty was loved by all
Who saw her standing there so tall

With accolades and eulogies they came
To share a moment with the lovely tree
To have their picture taken all in vain
Beneath its shade, in innocent simplicity
The people in the pictures did have names
But the tree had not, to no one's shame

It bore no fruit, so other trees could grow
No one thought to plant a mate beside it
Her seed had fallen aimlessly below
Her legacy of love was not provided
But fame and name yet came her way
For she was called, when her life had gone
The Hanging Tree of Nosegay

Trick or Treat

He was a treat I have to say, deliciously he came my way
Oblivious I was before, but now I thought I would explore
His obvious intentions, which I could not ignore
And I was oh so bored

He wanted to consume me, to wound me and entomb me
To whisk away my defense, to subdue my effervescence
His boldness had no pretense, which fed his very offence
For he was quite intense

I was at home, not all alone, entering my twilight zone
My stranger still in tow, his intentions all aglow
He petulantly crowed, of what he could bestow
As if I didn't know

A little wine, a little time, for inhibitions to subside
He was a credit to his kind, a beast of burden so inclined
To do the task he was assigned, surrendering his mind
The victim of his crime

Alas he had grown old to me, no more a curiosity
His function terminated, for which he was created
His essence subjugated, his future now was slated
As only death awaited

You see he had to pay, and bade me not delay
Forgive me he had pled, when chained upon my bed
For I rather now be dead, than be inside your head
A cruel trick, he said

Undying Love

I pretended to lie as she always believed me completely
She said she was a pear, existing out there, all by herself
She hung herself without affair, so neatly and discreetly
Her body swung in perfumed air, poignantly yet sweetly
I took her down and put her there, upright upon a shelf
As do swear, I sat and dared that she improve her health

She changed her mind relentlessly most every single day
And changed her scent religiously unfailingly quite daily
But never did she ask to change her clothes in any way
She begged me let her down, and promised not to stray
She then concertedly amused me, cavorting oh so gaily
But sadly dancing all around, she fell about most frailly

She wouldn't eat at any time, no matter what was made
And soon it was apparent, her figure had become too thin
I hung her back upon the tree that stood outside the glade
Her happiness returned, while back and forth she swayed
I knew she loved it there, for she revealed that little grin
Her love for me now unconcealed, as it had always been

Heed in Deed

Does a spirit know its fate?
Intangibles they are
Erasable at any rate
The thought is so bizarre

Are they in fact anomalies?
Impossible to know
Effectively it's only me
Their therapy I undergo

They speak to me in certitude
That it will come to pass
And I believe they do allude
That karma does amass

Alone it's me I must decide
Intangibles in fact exist
To let my conscious be my guide
Not fall in the Abyss

It's obvious, I'm not there now
And I don't want to be
But as for you, I pity you
If you refuse your therapy

Expose Yourself

Who are you to read my poem
Expecting to invade my home
Its sanctity right on display
To catch my soul in disarray

You feed upon the negative
You only take and never give
Integrity you call your own
But never wrote a single poem

Repulsively on love you feast
You hideous demonic priest
And gorge yourself on ridicule
You nasty literary ghoul

I know that I will never see
A critic with a soul to be

Nighty Night

First it comes as a whisper, carried by the winds of time
Enticingly the great elixir, calls unto thee to be entwined
In cosmic skies enshrined, in heaven's will to be nobility
In all things past or yet to be, embracing infinite capacity

As twilight time evokes an apprehensive contemplation
Vesperically you wonder, beseeching mortal vindication
In the dissipation of the day, surrendering its dominance
In natural gracious dignity, yielding all preponderance

Patiently you dwell amidst the ambiance of dusky lights
And contemplate the vagueness of your nugatory plight
You welcome time to whisk away the clutter all around
To take advantage of the night, to gain insight profound

Then clarity in flecks appear against the pitch black sky
You surrender unto Morpheus in hope you'll be revived

Decisions

Am I Awake? No matter
I can't eradicate my state
Those fire burning clocks
That tic tock all the time
Neatly hanging above me
Waiting to be noticed not

The xylophone of bones
And metered metronomes
Play in measured disarray
Black taping, taping notes
Tap rhythmically on wire
As the cadence never stops
The tic tock of the clocks

The constant rhyme of time
The minutia of your mind
All those countless clowns
Drowned in casks of wine
Sublime their cries escape
To the tic tock of the clock

I think I will have the soufflé

Severed

I was assigned to stand there, to bear there, wind and rain
I stood there stark and in the dark to mark my place in vain
The wind it blew and through and through, I full well knew
I was the one who had become, the someone who was due

Not a star in the sky to tell me why, I had to make this date
I can't bemoan my creaking bones, alone I knew my fate
In wet regrets and dampened threats and subtitle retribution
I felt the trickle from a bloodless sickle, in final execution

No song was sung while it was done in brutal callousness
Without a simper, or even a whimper, I fell in the abyss
I had become the very next one, to be attritioned and alone
An unknown corpse, a virtual drone, tagged to be disowned

No sympathetic epithets were whirled about in adoration
For it's not a joy to be employed by a giant corporation

I Ain't An Ant!

The ant trail was congested,
Or was I being tested?
Was I in line? Was I behind?
About to be molested?

Should I simply just speed up?
Or perhaps I should slow down?
Maybe surrender?
Nolo contendere?
Or prepare to leave the town?

Oh my God, what do I see?
Is that another ant by me?
Trying to escape?
Fearing to be raped?
Yielding all integrity?

Do you think that it is wise?
Will it hasten my demise?
To now confess? Like all the rest?
And just pay homage to the hive?

Passion

To feel passion is to taste of the fruits of love
Abandon ye all reason, to fly on winged doves
Taste the essence of ambrosia, sense the dare
You can smell the breath of sunshine in the air
It forces out the loathsome presence of despair

You can see beyond your selfish preservation
Acquire thoughts of ecstasy, be determination
Experience the energy you never knew before
Commit precociously, an act you can't afford
Dare to balance trust, submit before the Lord

Understand the gravity that spirits really fly
Embrace it candidly, your spirit's not inside
It's somewhere out there prodding you to be
Reject a rule embraced by mortals of insanity
For spirits fly translucently above impunity

What do they know of passion, all who die?
To only once have had it, is the reason why

Allured

Music was there
Beneath her breath
I could feel it
Upon my neck
T'was in her hair
Intertwined
Tuned in time
A breeze so fine
Bade me not
Resist
Play with me
She tickled
Wistfully so
Gently I did
Succumb
To then become
At peace with love

Just One Look

Frilly things that catch my eye do make me smile
Especially, when most attentively, I must surrender
Thoughts I had in mind, and lost to this contender
In the flicker of a moment, I could not reconcile
A reason not to look, that seemed to me worthwhile
Unashamedly I watched, to be the great defender
Of witnessing salaciously her show in all its splendor
For most assuredly I testify, the frilly thing had style

Consequences of this act should not be taken lightly
The sight you see can be the cause of your demise
To tread with caution, is the only way to brightly
Avoid a situation, where the intention is disguised
To lose your independent thought is quite unsightly
But desire trumping intellect, is simply no surprise

Souplexed

Chicken soup you need
To chase the cold away
And hardily I guarantee
I'll make it all the way

Egg noodles make it nice
And carrots give it flavor
As herbs will give it spice
A treat for you to savor

It's quite a healthy remedy
Whenever you are stricken
It's a cure for all humanity
But deadly to the chicken

An Amicable Resolution

Independence is my name and surely all the same
I'm packaged differently as you can plainly see
For I'm the incarnation of impunity

Don't think you can command or even reprimand
My nature to abide to rules you have prescribed
To try to subjugate my pride

I'm capable of everything and do most anything
It's inherent that I pounce upon the errant Mouse
For tenacity is me, ounce for ounce

Okay, so I am finicky, indeed perhaps persnickety
But for a special treat, a loving culinary feat
I'll pretend to be your Cat Elite

The Internet Cowboy

For I am the internet cowboy, and I don't just horse around
There's nothin' better I enjoy, than ridin' in to cyber town

When I saddle up my laptop, and I get my Stetson right
Giddy up I say, let's get it on, cause I'll be here all night

It's how now, cyber cows, when I come to your town
I scope 'em and rope 'em, -and then I stoke 'em
And make 'em feel glory bound

You can never mistake a CGI steak, it ain't even meat you can eat
I don't give 'em a break and I don't hesitate, when I hit that key delete

I have to have my women real, and buckaroo, this is the deal
Those chicks in bits got no appeal, this dude can really feel

It's how now cyber cows, when I come to your town
I scope 'em and rope 'em,- and then I stoke 'em
And make 'em feel glory bound

So let's make it clear, what good's a beer, when it ain't got no taste
Its suds and buds that's in my blood and that's what I call interface

When virtual regrets are all you get, when lookin' for some love
And e-mail and twitter just didn't deliver a cowboy from above

You drop me a line and I'll make you feel fine
And this cowboy will show up on time

For, it's how and now you cyber cow, when I come to your town
For, I'll scope ya and rope ya, -and then I'll stoke ya
And make you feel glory bound

Malaise

Pushing up daisies, one by one
Just doesn't seem to be much fun
I want to be on top again
Unfettered, to be naturally free
To cultivate a flowered destiny
To spindle and to bend
In wind and rain and sunny days
To bloom again and be amazed
And now I must contend again
Pushing up daisies one by one
Just doesn't seem to be much fun

Love's Demands

Love is many things, but it is not reality; it is a state of mind
That drives the machinery, the mechanics of dreams, forward
Both a curse and a blessing, love wields its awesome power
Equally transcending all time in a vengeance, second to none
It is the greatest fear in the cosmos, for it cannot be controlled
So insidious, its nature can and has subdued the mightiest of all
Innately born, it can't be stopped by knowledge or in ignorance
Even hate can be subdued by love, as fleeting as it seems to be
It appears with no apparent cause, to conquer unaquivolely
It can't be taught like hate, to lie and hide in terms of fate

In all its forms it has no shape and no dimension of existence
To make its presence known, evoking passion with impunity
Consequences be damned, as ecstasy is crowned omnipotent
Existentially existing betwixt desire and intellect it osculates
Our senses to spawn compelling action from our dormancy
Giving rise to thoughts of consternation, seeking now to ratify
Your past belief that your nature was content to be in peace
As the exhilaration of its power compromises your integrity
Adrenalized, your mortal being casts off its shackles joyously
From being trapped within its own mortality to rise above itself
And claim the prize of satisfaction to only linger momentarily
Basking in the deceitful afterglow that you have prevailed
In boasting to yourself to have entrapped the elusive love alive
As the folly of your existence makes you shudder deep inside
For kindness is not a quality of love, and neither is endurance
Evading definition, while hope, the scourge of man, prods on
The duplicity of which inevitably reveals its merciless ways
Denying everlasting rapture in cloaked amaranthine deception
Duplicity thy name is mine, love contumaciously propounds
To all who seek a taste come by, to may or not, be recognized
To risk your sacred soul, surrendering your cognitive control
Unto the soul of all who came before and who'll be thereafter
As I, the love of God, the greatest gift to man, command you
Give unto me assistance, for I alone cannot conceive mortality

Printed in the USA
CPSIA information can be obtained
at www.ICGtesting.com
LVHW021916061023
760082LV00018B/30